Dan Propper

E TALE OF THE AMAZING TRAMP

THE TALE OF THE AMAZING TRAMP

DAN PROPPER

CHERRY VALLEY EDITIONS

First edition

Calligraphy by Peter Strickman.
   Chinese character for 'Nothing'.

23 of these poems have been published in various
issues of: *Apple, Artists/U.S.A., Coldspring Journal,
Evergreen Review,* the *S.F. Good Times, Invisible
City, Longhouse, Love Lights, Moving On,* the *S.F.
Phoenix, Poetry Now, Provincetown Review, San
Francisco Gallery, San Francisco Review, Second
Coming,* the Albuquerque *Sun, Workshop,* and
Invisible City. My thanks to the editors.
                                          dp

This publication was made possible by
a grant from the National Endowment for the Arts,
a federal agency, in Washington, D.C.

Library of Congress Cataloging in Publication Data:
Propper, Dan, 1937-
   The tale of the amazing tramp.

   I. Title.
PS3566.R674T3   811'.5'4   76-58849
ISBN 0-916156-20-6

Typeset by Ed Hogan/Aspect Composition,
66 Rogers Ave., Somerville, Mass. 02144

Printed in the United States of America

ᴮLE OF CONTENTS

THE TALE OF THE AMAZING TRAMP

FOR RITA

VIEW II

The moon is up:
in the valley the river gleams,
burnished silver;
a train crosses a miniature
bridge, stitching with light;
on the far side, the mountain
looms up against the sky.

The train moves out of sight,
leaving the moon and the river
—then all is / lost to view:
the car / sweeps around a curve:
in the headlights
the broken dotted line
goes rushing by
like music
—in the glowing of the moon
the road is a white ribbon
cleanly stretched between
the two high walls of trees.

4/59

MORNING POEM FOR W.C.W.

slowly
the first   faint
haze of light

seeps upward   weakening

the moon's
electric brilliance

fading it
to butter-white

body of the river
comes to view

—the trees emerge
from black

to darkly-shadowed
green

—the birds
begin to call

(chilly
delicate-as-crystal
sounds

in lacy air)

light spreads

the moon
is wasted to a
dull grey wisp

—cannot reach
the river

—pale reflections
drift away

(copper light
settles down upon
the surface)

(the trees pulsate
green, green)

—the birds begin
conversing freely

an orange rim of sun
appears and rises

piled clouds
are touched with pink

and hang like
ornaments

perfumes rise up

pastel faces
are revealed

the sky is
washed with light!

things are seen and
heard with perfect
clarity! brightness!

air from the river
moves through
the young leaves

the first warm
tongue of morning
licks my face

noon is
centuries away

the birds
create an uproar

5/59

13

DEATHS

So another summer winds to an end,
and this, this August, green
and raucous in the sun, a season of death.
Bud Powell, Lenny Bruce, Boyd Raeburn, Frank O'H
One weekend.
Bud, specter and genius of Be-Bop,
retired from Paris and junk,
done with the semi-permanent
delicate paranoid balances of post-American
breakdown and ennui (futility)
—dead in Kings County Hospital
of Alcoholism and T.B.;
Boyd Raeburn, of heart-attack
somewhere on the Gulf, obscure, harried,
a businessman, nobody's ever heard of him
or his band (even Kenton and Herman
almost mythological now);
Lenny sprawled on cold tile bathroom-floor O.D.,
Hippies' Canyon, L.A., that good
Mexican Brown catches so many New York doojers;
I saw Frank 3 or 4 days before he was killed,
corner of 10th and C, had just re-read
his book on Jackson Pollock, and we
talked a moment. Pollock dead 10 years
this August, also by car and on Long Island;
now, ten years later, O'Hara run down
on the beach, and there is less than 100 acres
of usable building area left available in
Nassau County, Long Island an unbroken mass
of suburbia, solid houses from banal Mineola
to last gasp of Suffolk County line,
Suffolk itself domestic and thriving,
happily cutting its own throat,
boosting, wheeling, dealing, a giant turnip farm
—they're talking about a bridge to Connecticut
and a dam of the Sound
—supermarkets spring like mushrooms
—everything conceivable is named after
Walt Whitman (the Walt Whitman Bridge
and the Walt Whitman Dam).
That last time, O'Hara
never even made it to the surf.

8/66

14

NEW YORK BLUES

If I want some green
the whole town's on yellow.
When I was strung out on blue
they were all holding pink.
I know of an entire building
where everybody's alternately
dropping black and white:
they'd gladly lay some on me.
I don't want anything to do
with them cats.

5/67

SONG FOR ALAN WATTS

Nobody knows
exactly, where
yellow becomes green
except, perhaps
the Light Show Man
and no one can
delineate
the micro-infinitesimal
point at which
green turns
into blue
except perhaps
Miles Davis
but everyone can tell
where blue changes
to yellow
—that one's easy
can't you guess?
It's where
trees tune in
it's where
birds turn on
it's where
stars drop out.
You call me Precious
—I'll kick you
in your Zen.

5/67

PSALM 13

Now let all illuminated souls gather, unite, and
        rejoice, for the Holy Spirit, arisen, is
        striving to o'erspread the triple-levelled
        consciousnesses of the multitudinous human
        beings of this world.

How can it be denied?

Who could deny the vastness of the struggle now
        underway, infusion of bliss throughout the
        rigid-seeming but actually violently-
        resistant forms of human culture?

All signs hearten, indications presage imminent
        total victory by the forces of Ecstatic Being.

It is our portion to await, to praise and celebrate,
        to pray the coming of the molten, gold-
        illumined Eternity, and to further its
        arrival by being our most genial, generous,
        and loving, creative selves, and by staying
        as high as we possibly can.

1/12/68

SLOW SEQUENCE

From Chatauqua and Cattaraugus Counties of upper
New York State rise the Ischua and Tunnungwani
Creeks; which, passing the Cornplanter Indian
Reservation, form the headwaters of the Allegheny
River; which winds down through Pennsylvania and
at Pittsburgh runs into the Monongahela and forms
the Ohio; Big O, pushing, moving, moving down,
Cincinnati, Louisville, and Cairo, Illinois,
where it joins the Old Man, the Mississippi;
already wide as the length of an airport, at
St. Louis the Mississippi picks up the Missouri,
doubles its size, and starts its long slide
down the continent, one thousand miles, past
Memphis, Vicksburg, Natchez, Baton Rouge and
New Orleans, as heavy as pregnancy itself, come
all the long way down, rooted from Idaho to New
York, and now, laden with ships, set sunken in
its vast swampy delta ninety miles south of New
Orleans, canopied with mosquitos, enters the
greasy shallow mud-puddle of the Gulf, rushing
and roiling and dissipating, spreading outward,
washing and swirling around the pillars and the legs
of the ravening multitude of clustered oil rigs.

2/3/68

A CHAGALL (#1)

A Blue Circus,
a spotlight, and a red girl
swinging in the air,
illuminated, twisting,
face and breasts and buttocks
all facing you, you'd
really find it hard
to believe, except
it's supernormal compared
to the floating green donkey
she's facing, and the blue carp
who holds a bouquet,
floating above her, and
a blue chicken
with a yellow bill
resting upon her leg.
There's a radiant yellow sun
which contains a white crescent
moon with an eye, and a violin,
the moon may be playing it,
you can't be sure,
and other people, dancing,
hanging, twirling, spinning
hoops and playing violins,
and a green beautiful boy
who could be a Samurai
or the son of God,
vague among green leaves.

7/2/68

A CHAGALL (#5)

A mermaid! Oh sweet
Christ Almighty,
a mermaid, and
with red hair!
And floating in air,
no water, high above
a line of date palms,
high above a road
and a row of houses,
and high above
a floating fish
himself above
everything else
except the sun,
gently holding
a huge bouquet of
flowers, red, yellow,
and white, they float too,
and her tail
yellow, orange,
white and blue,
and white clouds
in a pale ultramarine sky,
barely delineated,
and large titties,
she has giant
straight-thrusting titties,
you'd never believe them
on a girl, let alone
a mermaid.

7/2/68

BLUE POLES

Blue Poles
stand in a magic circle,
feathered, ragged as clouds,
rigid, though leaning
each its own way, as if
vulnerable to any wind;

structuring an atmosphere
of paint,
and a world of paint,
and a universe
of painting, and the life
of a man now dead,
forever alive.

Miro blue, white swirling
sunk in darkness, yellow
resplendent as the fire
of the sun, Blood Red!
It is a savage rite.

Blue Poles standing
in a spread circle, rigid
and feathery, ragged
and vulnerable, leaning
in a whirlwind of paint.

And the I Ching says
number 50, The Caldron
change number 11, Peace.

Sweet tempest!
            —like
watching Casals, 93 and
roaring leonine Tchaikovsky
at the young orchestra.

                          1/6/70

21

IF   everything you perceive is miraculous
THEN you are in a state of Grace

IF   you get there
THEN you will like it

IF   you don't realize your happiness until afterw
THEN you are a normal dumbbell and the joke is o

ALL THIS   is in itself miraculous

5/18/70

FOR LEARY ON THE LAM

We're all tripping now it's the big move
First David Jansen the good fugitive
Then Ben Gazzara on borrowed time
Those two dopes on route 66
Wagon train up Reagan's ass
Mediamen trekking to the rites of
                    J.E. Hoover's Witnesses
Allen went to India we all went too
Kesey all around and up and down
Too much speed blew Cassady away, really
                        too bad
Jack on the road and on a train and on a ship
      wine slowed him down, as it must
Now we have Romney in a caravan
      Hollywood's Waviest Gravy
And then came Bronson goodbye
People tripping to jails, Vietnam too
Partridge Family tripping to the meat machine
      orange bus all full of Partridges
Trippin' the Chisolm Trail
      with saintly ol' uncle John Wayne, hi-yo
Easy Riders splattering the fields
Rubber engineers walking on the moon
Waiting for Nixon to trip across his Rubicon

                    9/14/70

SIGNBOARD

THE GOOD TIME
ROLLIN', REELIN', ROCKIN',
SWAYIN', STAGGERIN', STUMBLIN',
MUMBLIN', BABBLIN', HOWLIN', MOANIN',
RANTIN', RAVIN', LEAPIN', STOMPIN',
SHIVERIN', SHAKIN', DANCIN', QUAKIN',
LAUGHIN', SHOUTIN', SINGIN',
WHOOPIN', HOLLERIN',
BELLERIN' LIKE A BULL CALF
AN' TALKIN' IN TONGUES
IN PRAISE OF OUR FATHER IN HEAVEN
AND CELEBRATION OF OUR MOTHER THE EA
—COME ON IN HERE WITH US!—
BLESSED TEMPLE OF THE SUBLIME HOLY SPI
AND ETERNAL WELL OF BLISS AND AMAZIN(
INFINITE MIRACULOUS POWER SANCTIFIED (

11/14/71

24

THE TALE OF THE AMAZING TRAMP

(for Father Dan Berrigan)

My character is pretty stable, I
stay much the same from day to day,
liking the same kind of humor, the
same sorts of food, the same type of sex;
but inside me is a gigantic opera,
with hundreds of characters,
and lots of them are going at once
in a mad divine ecstatic rant:
there's a wild turned-on holyrollin'
dancin' snakekissin' preacher-man,
oh yes, couldn't get along without him;
there's an old Jew who sees it all,
and understands the hassles
everyone goes through, and groans to God
"Oh, woe is me! Tell me how I can
help the people!"
and feels helpless, and powerless
—he's Jesus' sad daddy, I guess
I need him too;
there's a wild young sailor
who gets roaring drunk in every port,
gives all his money away to the whores
and calls them Sister and charms
the hell out of 'em, and even though
he's broke now, still he manages
to wake up in some lady's bed,
because he's sincere, hookers
value that, they can always tell;
let's talk about The American Dream:
"I want to grow up and be a Pig.
I want to have three of everything
and enough left over so that I
never have to worry, because I'm terrified.
I want to lay around drunk all day,
oblivious, and never do any work
but once in a while go out and yell
at the workers, order 'em around,
and I wanna shit on everything,
I refuse to bury my turds, I insist
upon leaving a trail of pollution,
and I'm gonna rip up the earth
and root out the life and eat it up,
and when I die I'll leave a trail

of waste and desolation they'll
talk about a thousand years!"
Cheer up, friends, that song
is hardly ever performed, Thank God.
Hey there's a beautiful innocent Poet,
watching the falling leaves, weeping.
He's surprisingly lots of trouble to keep,
but I think he's worth it.
Hitler is there too, but it's alright
because I've forgiven him;
he's an old, sad, tired man,
sits in a corner never speaking.
There's a cop who's mad at everybody,
he wants 'em all to obey the laws
or else he'll hit 'em with his club,
he's very upset, in fact he's
constantly disturbed, I suspect
he doesn't really want to be a cop,
what he really wants to do is go fishing,
and play with his children and drink beer,
get a card in the carpenters' union
and live a normal life. Pray for him.
There's King Kong, stompin' up the street
tearin' up everything, oh no it's
just that pesky Pig,
tryna break into Show Biz;
here's a wildass 1947 Bebop musician
one of the world's great hipsters,
he lives on benzedrine and plays
fantastic saxophone 24 hours a day,
every note is a miracle and even just
the sound of his horn itself is mesmerizing,
a man came three thousand miles
just to buy him a hot dog,
our boy paid his trainfare back, and smiled.
Oh and this is a fine young Taoist
Christian Marxian Anarchist who wants to
gently remove the toys from the children's
hands before they hurt themselves,
he's all heart, like they say, but dumb,
no sense of tactics, he's on his way
to an intellectual farm in Vermont;
hey here's a real American Cowboy,
got a vocabulary of 47 curses
and thirteen words in Horse,
he's usually either drunk or in a cast,

a nice person, makes friends easily,
he'd be a big help on that farm;
oh, and some more Heroes:
this one got gassed in the First
World War, he's a vegetable;
this one came ashore at Iwo Jima
with his pants full, that day
bayonetted a Jap whose scream
he still hears twice a week in dreams,
almost thirty years now he wonders
if somewhere there's a person
with a bayonet for him;
this one froze his toes in Korea;
this one had his tool blown off in 'Nam
and came back with a monkey 30 feet tall;
it was nuthin' Ma, nuthin' at all.
Here's some more guys you know:
Joe Polack and Sam Spade and Tommy Mick
and Angelo, you remember them,
they built the cities, in fact,
it was probably you, chicken coops
to Empire State to Golden Gate,
most likely it was you all along, Citizens.
Well I've talked a long time and my throat is dry,
so bless you all, friends, and for now goodbye.

3/1/72

THE ANNIHILATION OF JAIL

No man can be put into Jail
so long as he stands and declares himself Free.
No citizen who declares himself Free
can have his Freedom taken from him.
This is the great weapon of the people.
No concrete walls, no inch-thick bars of steel,
can capture what is alive and Free within me.
No arguments can persuade me
to feel guilty, dirty, or wrong.
I move from an inner surety and righteousness
compared to which the existing legal system
is mongoloid idiot drool.
Put me down into your lowest, dankest hole,
and I can and will dream and surpass it.
I declare the annihilation of Jail!
I declare the annihilation of Jail!
I declare the annihilation of Jail!
Shanti. Shanti. Om Shanti. Padme Hum.

4/24/72

THE PHASES OF THE MOON

The hypomanic pizza does a wheelie up the hill
upon its tiny pepperoni discs;

a field of asparagus achieves a horrible catharsis;

the suicidal tadpole mounts the vomiting rhinoceros
under the glinting light of a springtime quarter-moon;

the aurora borealis has carnal knowledge of an
adolescent cantaloupe.

We must reform the unreliable trolleycars;

we must unload the dubious bananas;

we must disarm the aching schizophrenic ennui-process,
and attend the concrete watermelon's genuflections.

(The weekend vivisectionist argues with
the herbivorous meatball;

a brigade of trained fleas dictates a road-map
over the telephone.)

5/13/72

29

MESSAGE TO THE UNITED NATIONS

I want the flags torn loose from the thunder
in the full sun of day, at the zenith,
in a hush, as steam rises in the greenhouses
and birds are struck mute by the heat;

I want the thunder torn from the tongue of the sun
and buried in the sea,
as children's marching-bands play out of tune
waving all their tinsel, their spangles and flags;

I want the thunder and the flags together burned
by a towering lens reflecting the sun,
a bowl of emerald, sapphire, and gold,
a paradigm of brightness,

and I want them swallowed forever
in the immense vertigo of hurled fire,
moribund salamander no longer able to rise:

and then, from the blazing center of the flames,
from the dizzying height of the incandescence,
a parade of lightning-strokes
silently to emerge in awesome serried rows,

proclaiming the Power in the universe
to humble the maddest of men,
dissolving the obscene dialectics of the generals,
obliterating all the configurations of politics

and welcoming the beatific lion whose mercy
sustains the people, the lion of Samson
in the stead of the lion of Nemea
vanquished by once-mad Heracles finally and foreve

and then, at last, the dissolution of ranks
in the regiments of slavery
as the people re-emerge from their sleep
and come forward in a vast alive frontier,

in a hurricane of souls born again
in the silent thunderclap of the leaves,
in the sapient amplitude of the conflagration!

10/2

30

ODE TO THE CINEMA

(for Nathaniel West)

The huge images
move upon the immense white screen:
we are at the movies, and there is conflict.
Always there is conflict at the movies,
and we sit, large replicas
of the animals we once were as children,
and we laugh, and weep, and scream,
and we pick our noses, and we
stuff ourselves with incredibly tempting
useless food, and we throw everything
on the floor, because we are At The Movies.

Look! Cardinal Richelieu plots again!
Look! A gigantic manlike beast
rises from the swamp and
crunches human beings like radishes!
Look! Moses sees God, accompanied
by an organ. Look again! It's God Himself,
played by Charlton Heston.

Look again! Look again!
The movies go on, the movies are eternal.
What's playing at the movies?
The Movies are playing at the movies!

Did you know that the insane asylums
are full of people who think
they're Napoleon? Napoleon himself
thought he was Jesus. Jesus, in turn,
thought that he was God.
What does God think?
Where does it all end?
It ends in the Movies!

Here! The cavalry is massacring the Indians!
Here! The Indians are torturing a soldier!
Here, a friendly old priest
is spooning soup into an exhausted alcoholic.
Here, for some reason, is a close-up
of the world's biggest pair of tits!

The show's only begun: here's "Romeo And Juliet"
played by Joe Namath and Barbra Streisand!
Here's the United Nations, played by John Carradin
Here's "The Invisible Man", played by The Holy Gh
Joan Crawford and the Houston Philharmonic
starring in "Sodom And Gomorrah"! What a show!

The endless figures parade across the immense
panorama of the screen, immortal, impassioned,
and compassionate upon the vast horizon.

Here's a torrential storm lashing
the fear-crazed natives of a paradisical isle!
Here! Surrounded by oafs, dolts, and louts,
a solitary genius invents the wheel!
Icarus flies! Ulysses trips!
Get another bag of peanuts,
we haven't seen anything yet!
Here comes the Pelloponnesian War!
There's "The Conquest of Peru", in E-flat.
Ben Franklin and Thomas Jefferson
are drinking ale in Cinemascope.
Are you tired? Here's a nice nostalgic
Faulknerian story about stomping around
in the woods, in the rain, drunk,
carrying shotguns and mumbling something
or other about Niggers and Yankees.
Here's The World's Handsomest Man,
and his wife, The World's Most Beautiful Woman,
and their love for each other,
The World's Most Perfect Example Of Love.

Here, in the dark palace of dreaming,
in the cushioned, insulated, encapsulate
nave of the imagination, is gentleness,
ferocity, courage, love, honor, magnanimity,
hatred, arrogance, jealousy, lust,
cowardice, humility, stupidity, cruelty,
vengefulness, mercy, and righteousness!
Here is ecstasy and shame!

Here is a man attacking a woman
with a gigantic knife! Here is a woman
attacking a child with a cup of acid!
Here is a child attacking a village
with burning gasoline!, at the movies.

Here's a documentary: President Kennedy
is being shot, again, and again, and again,
in slow-motion, in grainy close-ups,
at normal speed. Here's World War II,
with Glenn Ford, Richard Widmark,
John Wayne, Richard Jaeckel, Alan Ladd,
Frederick March, Gregory Peck,
Robert Mitchum, Clark Gable,
William Holden, Trevor Howard, and Lassie.
Here're the Jews wandering in the desert
40 years, it only takes 3 minutes.

Here's Franklin Delano Roosevelt saving America,
and Winston Churchill saving England, and
Josef Stalin saving Russia, and Adolf Hitler
saving Germany, and Kwame Nkrumah saving Ghana,
and Chiang Kai Shek saving China, and Fidel Castro
saving Cuba, DeGaulle saving France, Nasser
saving Egypt, and Ho Chi Minh saving Vietnam
at the movies, at the movies,
at the movies, at the movies, at the movies!

Children, let me slip it to you
really quick and gentle.
The Movies are merely a great opportunity
to holler "Theatre!" in a fiery crowd.

Do you want to see God?
Don't look in the movies,
because God absolutely
does not go to the movies.
If you had any sense, neither would you.

Tonight? Tonight is
Marlon Brando and Anna Magnani
in "The Ramayana". Hurry up,
we don't want to miss the beginning.

11/30 - 12/7/72

LITTLE WILLIE LEAPS

(Charlie Parker, Savoy LP 1200

You know when Little Willie's high,
'cause Little Willie whistles, and he dances,
and at times he leaps right up into the sky!
, and people who can dig it are affected by his prese
grandmas, kids, and dogs, and even a hypnotized po
catch a soupcon of exuberance
and smile, and bounce benignly on their way.

(This flash reverberates in the street as he passes by,
and it lingers a moment more:
ambience of salubrity!)

And Willie knows his mental worth:
he's cognizant of mirth as both a poultice and a balr
to soothe the harried heads he meets;
so Willie dances, happy, down the streets of his city,
whistling Bop and manifesting all of his mental treas
as he smiles and says "Hello my man!",
and contemplates some chocolate ice-cream.

No dream:
the soul expands and glows
as Little Willie leaps!

1/6/73

34

ONE, TWO, MANY POETRY READINGS

Always three in red and six in black;
always at least one lined face;
always a few on display;
usually a headache, and absolutely always
a hangover;
2 or 3 God-struck ones,
2 blond kids hoping to get laid,
6 ex-junkies, 4 homosexuals,
17 bi-sexuals, and 2 sad celibates;
possibly four with talent, all
secretly knowing themselves the nation's greatest;
always two dropped-out musicians:
"I used to play alto",
"I played drums";
one ex-beauty, one nervous lady with short hair,
one male late-adolescent sexual posturer;
always a babbling refugee from hallucinogens;
one with a long poem called "The Ultimate List",
one meshugineh talking about corduroy tulips,
and one Visiting Star.

1/18/73

POEM FOR THE END OF THE YEAR

Ulysses, with his feet like flounders
and his arms like pianos,
comes home smiling
from his trip across the frying-pan,
worships the acacia, the pomegranate,
the almond and the lemon, and becomes
a Greek sponge-fisherman
with a name like a machine-gun
that translates, "Tom Sawyer",
and children named Socrates
and Aphrodite, and a wife
building fires on the shore
at night, to cheat Poseidon,
he whom the Romans called Neptune
called Old Man in our own South

—where Hemingway
fought his Ahab of a plot at sea,
and fought devils
in a cathedral of booze
—or Steinbeck's drunken Danny
at the ravine of demons
—or Malcolm Lowry
stoop-shouldered standing on his
wharf at Lethe, propitiating
some mad god, throttled by enigmas.

Mars and Neptune struggle
in the great combing
of the rocks in the surf,
(Pisces on the cusp of Aries).

Even after the Nobel, there still
were people in Oxford
who thought of Faulkner as the town drunk:
that chaste, chivalric angel!
(Volcanoes are as nothing only to Apollo.)

BENEDICTION:
Let us raise the green banner
with the white dove; let us
nail it to the mast
and sail off in every direction,

leaving Bismarck, and platinum,
and Bacchus, and Pan, and
the murder of Rosa Luxemburg
behind; let us issue stamps
with red birds and green beetles on them,
in commemoration of nothing but themselves;
stamps with yellow flowers and ships
under sail; stamps with impalas,
mushrooms, butterflies, and fishermen.
Let us carry the lamps through the wheat field.

                    3/20/73

FOR NERUDA

Picasso just dead its Lenins birthday
today what a hell of a way to start a poem
Aries and the moon just went into Leo
Im an Aries and me Venus is in Aries too
a walking sexbomb
                                but its a beautiful
bright blue sunshine day in San Fran
and Id rather make poetry
          start with lovemaking jeez the
changes will get us there sooner or later
          the moral code we as adults
to become adults must sooner or later lay out
          should we be so fortunate as to grow up
will almost inevitably include giving
as equal to or just slightly less important than
or maybe even more important than receiving
whatever and however it pays off lovemaking
sexual encountery with or without orgasm
everytime with increased tender awareness
          or forget all that jive
and live with the drowned ones in octopus
land in the solitude of the antediluvian
while outside it is bluegreen
flushed with yellow and the trees
have ears they have eyes they have fingers
which are leaves that funnel and track
precisely as animals or radar distributing
the sunlight and rain throughout the turf
and boundary of the treebeing
                                nourishing
and replenishing symbiotic helpmates
which absorb and live in the earth
in a protocol of survival
                    not to forget
the leaves themselves in the noontime
stillness and heat
drooping and resting and replenishing
          as a rustred hawk hangs in the air
concerned with the motionpatterns
of rodents
          and later on in the dark
an owl will perch and scan by ear
          and during the night the moon

is a great illuminated clock descending
through the towering trees
                          and the trees
drink and eat their food of the day
and feed the leaves as well
                          and the leaves
catch the wind and massage the trees
yes indeed friends the simmering
expendable lashing exacerbated diaphonous
membranes
                    actually snare the wind
and indeed they do massage the trees
        and the trees have stomachs and thighs
and arms and hearts
                          and they graze
similar to cattle and primordial plankton
        and they are capable of joyousness
and panic and great patient striving
        and the trees have spirits this
is not a game it is the Great Spirit
Wakan Tanka which allows me to know this
        the Great Spirit which the spirit
of each tree is of
        as the spirit of myself is of it
                    and a Footnote
one can spend years reading books sutras
discourses parchments inscribed stones
and ancient scrolls
                    there are gurus to follow
universes of honey and purgatories of wasps
        one can study the singing of Lady Day
from the old recordings made when her voice
was still dedicated and masterful
        one can camouflage oneself in a cloak
of rationality
                    or mindless natural living
or mindless imagistic lust
                          and of course
there is always your lifetime supply
of opiates available at immensely wretched
dismal deteriorative spiritual effort
        or one can sit for 42 years
contemplating a rusty ballbearing
        myself I ride the eidetic carousel
of the racial unconscious
                          and I try

to recognize and signal that Great Spirit
which I am of
                    and to live with trees
and resplendent people and poems
and ecstatic animals and music
and flowers and painting and every thing
in its gemlike and probably unaware
perfection
          I live with trees at my window
I live with Wakan Tanka as he permits me

                              4/10/73

FOR BOB BRANAMAN, LAWRENCE LECLAIR
AND PETER STRICKMAN, PAINTERS

The sea hurls itself upon itself,
patient and imperial; the wind
thunders against the waves
in a grandiose gesture of violence.
The rabbi who spoke eight times
in forty years, upon one of these
occasions said: "The Lord Is One.
Blessed is he who understands
the meaning of this phrase,
'The Lord Is One' "
                    , and a hundred
years later ecstatic Hassidim are
dancing into their graves, singing
in the ovens, and we have
The Unified Field Theory.
The mountains of the planet
crumble with infinitesimal magnitude
as the protein shortage approaches
crisis and money become totally abstract.
Only the light matters, and this is
not a pun on "E=MC/squared".
The light, and how it becomes matter.
Picasso knew this, Matisse and Cezanne
saw and painted it. Klee, Kandinsky,
Klimt. Kline. Arshile Gorky painted
cross-sections of Seraphim. Pollock
threw paint with the same furious faith
as Moses striking the rock.
The nation cries out in anguish,
frustration, and despair, as
the Bank of America burns in a
blooming petroleum glare, flaring
in the gloom of Bosch's unstable
firmament: orgasms and sobbing.
Rembrandt saw the same miracle
of light as was revealed to Van Gogh;
Chagall and Miro dance the identical
fandango (or is it a polka?);
Monet's water-lilies seen close up
are a pastiche of pink tombstones
—an anticipation of Mondrian
still to come, and later on,

41

DeKooning and Hartung and Hoffman
and the Standard Oil road-map
of the State of Iowa.
Tumultuous blasts rip the murk
surrounding the spires of America's
towering ego, as we devour ourselves
in the name of Usury.
                    Sail on, painters,
sail on, like Billy Budd still safe
aboard the good ship "Rights of Man".
Discard the anchor and take up the brush
like Quixote his rose and his sword,
in all your bursting, light-filled
excellence. The brush: to make:
"The Lord Is One!"

                              4/24/73

THE RAPE OF SOUTH AMERICA,
OR, TERMINAL SYMBOLISM
(for Judith Abrahms)

Uncle Sam rides up upon a huge, lumbering
armadillo, he waves his high hat in a
whoopee cowboy spiral and dismounts
a la Fred Astaire sweeping arm-flourish and bow,
and the natives are interested.
"Santa Maria!" mumbles a toothless old crone
as Uncle Sam passes out cans of bad pork and
pills and saran wrap, and makes a grandiose
speech promising wealth to everyone.
He whips out a .45 and shoots the armadillo
in the eye, and the natives pounce upon the corpse
for this meat their staple protein. Uncle Sam
bellows for them to halt but they devour the carcass.
A company of soldiers appears with their rifles
and cover the natives. Everyone freeze, and
Uncle Sam passes out can-openers, pacifying
the people, encouraging the women to take the pills
and the men to wrap their penises in plastic,
but the men and women trade, the men take all
the pills and the women drape themselves in
plastic wrap. Uncle Sam orders the troops to fire
but the people fight back, stabbing with their
can-openers, and soon everyone has been killed
but Uncle Sam, who screeches and fires his .45
into the air.

5/28/73

43

MODERN TIMES

Wall of white washing-machines
like an armada under full sail
just come over the horizon
but at this very moment something's
gone wrong: some stand a-gape
in the water, some are trembling,
some whizz like children's toys
that mystifyingly go nowhere, and
one whines to a halt like a jet;
one has been holed by a dreadnought's
shell and spews feathers and milky
soapwater like sloshy pudding
spilled all over the floor,
one pillow attempting to take its
tormentor with it into death
—and the entire fleet suddenly
caught short in the shoal-water,
up against the cliffs of the panorama
of tumbling dryers that line
the other wall, yellow and blank
like the bluffs of East Africa
—and a long table between, with
people methodically folding clothes,
or zombielike watching their loads
go 'round, or loaf outside
and scratch their bellies drinking coke
as the perpetrators of the pillow disaster
flee the scene like Masaccio's thunderous
Adam And Eve Fleeing The Garden.

6/30/73

44

TO MY ANCESTORS

What are the spiders ceaselessly weaving?

Why are the ants mining everywhere?

What is a child's doll doing in the Sahara,
or a rusted bomber in the jungle of Borneo?

Where is the joke that all the trumpet's glories
are based on the sound of a fart?

Why are redwood trees used to wipe asses?

Has one Lacondan indian ever read
"The Conquest of Peru"?

Why has this brain gone to the movies?

How come the railroad-wheels screech
only when the train is creeping?

How come the dropped bread
always lands butter-side down?

How come you never drop a hardboiled egg?

How come you never get a "busy" signal
when you've dialed a wrong number?

Why is the most exhilarating Jazz *The Blues*?

(Raggedy Andy breasts the waves
of the Antarctic.

Lost scrolls unfurl their gospels
in swamps without names.)

How many of us nightmare airplane-crashes
who never flew?

Where is the dancing school the clumsy
novice butterflies attend?

What city is this we are at home in
though never having seen it?

9/15/72 - 9/1/73

FOR NERUDA, FOR ALLENDE, FOR CHILE, FO

Don Pablo it's strange and noble
as the Spanish language
is strange and noble, and it's
Surrealistic in that wild Spanish
style extending back to "Don Quixote".

I have loved your work for years,
and admired you as a human entity,
but within the past month I've found
that the available translations
of your work are slipshod, and while
working furiously, (35 poems in 29 days),

there occurred the heart-stopping coup
of the Fascists in your country, and
the murder of your President, Senor Allende.

I have been planning this letter
for a few weeks to tell you that I now
love you as a man, *and* as a poet,
and I'm told it's too late: you "died"
three-or-four days ago, of "cancer",
while in "Protective Custody".
They will probably burn your books.

Don Pablo, I know that as a translator
of English literary works, you had
knowledge of how badly your own work
had been mistreated.

(The money rustles, the trees droop,
the crepescular fading happens,
the rats work incessantly,
the rivers polluted and the indians,
the copper and the nitrate
once again accepted
by the powers of sustenance)
, and you are with Vallejo,
with Lorca, with Jimenez.

You are dead of politics and I have
finished "Estravagario" and
"Las Piedras De Chile". Now I begin

on "Plenos Poderes", on the grapes,
the ice, the stones, the enigmas.

Childlike and playful as you,
I will hold up my hand
like the boy with his hare
on the highway. In the dark.

                              9/27/73

UNTITLED POEM

Pablo Picasso's birthday
today (he died this spring),
and three weeks ago Pablo Neruda
murdered by the Fascists,
and four days ago, on
the anniversary of Kerouac's death,
I said to my woman
Picasso and Neruda, all
they need now is Casals,
the bases loaded,
and yesterday Casals died.

Three Spanish Pablos,
all in a year, and
a hundred-thousand more,
unnoticed, mere peons
and underfed laborers.

Like Kerouac said in his
last drunken
trapeze-act of a book:
"Where is he tonight?
And I? And you?"

Where are the
hundred-thousand widows?
Where are their sons?
Who holds Ernesto Guevera's
rifle in his arms?

Oh friends, Eliot sank
in a sun-cracked dory
behind the altar, Pound
went mad in a cul-de-sac
of politics and money and
translations and denials of
his own intrinsic tenderness,
Williams worked his ass off
pulling fish-hooks from
the thumbs of the proles,
Mao is about to die,
the Arabs can't get it
together to wipe out the Jews,

and no good reason to anyhow,
Ginsberg and Kerouac
both queer in their fear
of having offspring
(Hindu anxieties),
the Vice-President out,
caught in his vices,
the President next and it
doesn't matter, the Army
takes it all, the Earth
our mother can't take
much more, and the true
revolution is the brown
babies as the races blend
—another hundred years and
we'll have a black Jewish Pope
who'll give all away,
if we can hang in there
—and the three Pablos are dead:

all that painting, all that poetry,
all that music, and THAT LIVES!
And the sweat
of the hundred-thousand unknown
Pablos: *that* lives:

and their formidable sons,
who shall yet redeem their
heritage of grapes and emerald
and bananas and coca
and sexuality from the mud:

crushing the rats, toppling
the towers, stoned on marijuana
in the public parks, in anarchistic
barbecues, in churches dedicated
to the Christ of the People,
on street-corners, in plaster
rooms, on the lawns.

10/25/73

FOR THE HIGH PRIESTS AT EASTER-TIDE

When we were green and passionate to empathize
man's gyring scope, we dared the sun's direct
blaze of our fathers' histories with our
dewy throbbing Christlike eyes, and slowly
photographed upon our hearts our ancient
convoluted maze of trails with all their
turnings, falterings, and momentary rests
of greed and envy, infantile random lusts
for power, rapes and murders, suicides
and grimy schemes and mad mute semi-conscious
sins which were our regal stumbling
godless heritage, our race's curse upon itself,
until our souls were shriveled by the heroic
immensity of the thwarted ancestral dreamings
and we returned from the encyclopedic odyssey
of misdirected fumbling lives with jumbled brains
like chestnuts charred, fit to dream of forcemeat,
violence, poisons, weapons, vengefulness
and pain, and fled the endless nightmare
from which there is no flight, and fled
as best we could from this infinitude of animals
wallowing their own excrement, ran toward
any semblance of sanity and love and light:
so now Jack meanders in a misty dank of alcohol,
and Billy stalks his shrinking veins with opiates,
and Michael's gone a convert to the filthy
thieving scheme, and lucky Joe's found Buddha,
and all the rest of us are fit for nothing more
than gaze with milky eyes at nothing,
and these the stations of the monetary cross:
tomorrow Christ is born again, and every day,
and it continues, for all save lucky Joe
and the blessed wealthy few who Know.

4/13/74

50

THE GODS

Hello; it's good to see you;
it's good to have you back again.
I know we know each other
almost three thousand years now,
but still, a half-year seems like
a century —let the longing,
in tandem with the consummation,
be the measure of my love.
—Shakespeare? —or did I just
make it up? It's difficult to say,
in this ballet of tenderness,
fatigue, and warmth. What's certain
is that the warm flesh revere
and enclose the warm flesh,
the brow be calm and unwrinkled
in the knowledge of the presence
of the other, the tongue cherish
the corporeal form —its other self,
its other half, its new-found
siamese, its counterpart
—sometimes twenty minutes is
a lifetime. As the Poet says:
"The warm bodies shine together,
the hand moves toward the center
of the flesh, the soul comes joyful
to the eye ..." Yes, and we are
once again become the treasure
and the wonderstruck discoverer,
posited upon this plane of joyous
interaction, turgid with our thirty
centuries' playful knowledge,
wise and helpful in our courteous
estimation of each other,
met delicate and graceful
in our latest dance beneath
the pale white banner
of the bird tree flower music moon!

5/26/75

51

The light as the light goes
is liquid, is
red and green and liquid,
from here
all the way across the valley
and most of the way up the hill
is under water;
that small white hawk
floats on the surface
way up there.

7/4/76

Peter Stroschen

DAN PROPPER grew up in Brooklyn, N.Y.
He began writing in 1956 at the age of 19,
and has had about 250 of his poems published
in many magazines. His poem, "The Fable of
the Final Hour", was included in Seymour
Krim's anthology, "The Beats", and has been
translated into 8 or so European languages.
This is his first book of poetry since "The
Fable of the Final Hour and other poems", in
1958. Since 1973 he has translated approxi-
mately 150 poems by Pablo Neruda of which
some 50 have been published in various magazines, and in his book, "Pablo Neruda: 23 Poems"
(Energy Press, 1977). He lives in the hills between the desert and the ocean, just north of
the Mexican border.

$2.50

Cherry Valley Editions
Box 303
Cherry Valley,
NY 13320

ISBN: 0-916156-20-6 $2.50

CHERRY VALLEY EDITIONS